To my sons Ares and Eros
To my nephews Alessandro and Allan
To my whole family, getting bigger!

A mis hijos Ares y Eros
A mis sobrinos Alessandro y Allan
A toda mi familia, ¡cada vez más grande!   –Y.C.

Dedicated to my BIG family—
my three brothers and my sister,
Brad, Jon, Tom, and Shanti   –M.A.

Reycraft Books
55 Fifth Avenue
New York, NY 10003
Reycraftbooks.com

Reycraft Books is a trade imprint and trademark of Newmark Learning, LLC.
Copyright ©2020 by Reycraft Books, an imprint of Newmark Learning, LLC

Educators and Librarians: Our books may be purchased in bulk for promotional, educational,
or business use. Please contact sales@reycraftbooks.com.

This is a work of fiction. Names, characters, places, dialogue, and incidents described either
are the product of the author's imagination or are used fictitiously. Any resemblance to
actual persons, living or dead, is entirely coincidental.

Library of Congress Cataloging-in-Publication Data is available.

ISBN: 978-1-4788-6790-6

Photograph credits: Jacket Flap A: CBHBooks/wikipedia.org; Jacket Flap B: John Rae Photo.

Printed in Guangzhou, China
4401/1119/CA21902021
10 9 8 7 6 5 4 3 2 1

First Edition Hardcover published by Reycraft Books

Reycraft Books and Newmark Learning, LLC, support diversity and the First Amendment,
and celebrate the right to read.

MY BIG FAMILY

written by
Yanitzia Canetti

illustrated by
Micha Archer

In my house, there are three of us—
Mama, Papa, and me.
I have a very big family, though.

"You have grandparents in Cuba," says Papa.
"And lots of aunts, uncles, and cousins,"
Mama reminds me.

One day, I notice Mama wearing her favorite shirt, and Papa singing while he makes empanadas.

Mama is looking at the photo album and showing me pictures I've seen again and again.

Papa tells the story of my grandmother Juanita
growing up in the little town in Cuba.
"Abuela's house had soaring, high ceilings," he says.
"And big, wide windows," Mama says.

Since I hear this story all the time,
I think they really want to tell me something else.

"Alex, how would you like it
if our family were bigger?"
Mama asks.

"Yes!" I shout. It would be nice
to have more family here.

"Well, guess what?" says Mama.
"Your grandmother is coming
from Cuba tomorrow!"

I jump up and we all hug.
I can't believe our family
is getting bigger!

"Where three
can fit,
four can fit,"
says Papa.

We pick up Abuela Juanita from the airport
and when we get home, I help Abuela
put her things in my room.
Now it is our room.

Luckily, everything fits—my dresser,
her bedside table, my toys,
her books, my drawing table,
her jewelry box, my bed, her bed.

And I'm glad she likes my room.
It looks like a planetarium.

The next morning, the phone rings.
I hear Mama shouting.
She sounds happy.

As soon as she hangs up, she runs
over to me.

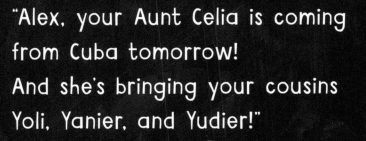

"Alex, your Aunt Celia is coming
from Cuba tomorrow!
And she's bringing your cousins
Yoli, Yanier, and Yudier!"

"Yes!" I say.
"The bigger,
the better."

Now there's never a quiet moment.

My cousins teach me new games.

We watch movies and

they make me laugh a lot.

In the kitchen, Abuela, Mama, and Aunt Celia cook Cuban food together.

Aunt Celia talks so loud
that Papa has to turn up
the TV to hear it.

But the smell
of garlic, onion,
and fried plantains
brings us all to
the table hungry.

After dinner, we take turns
sitting in the living room.
But when I stand up to stretch my legs,
Yudier plops down in
the most comfortable chair.
"You snooze, you lose!" he says.

Just then,
the phone rings.

Oh no!

I hear Mama yelling
happily again.
As soon as she hangs up,
she runs over to me.

"Guess what, Alex? Cousin Beto is coming to live with us, too!"

Papa just smiles.

"Where eight can fit, nine can fit," he says.

"No one else can fit in this house!"

In the morning, when it's time for breakfast,
everyone wants something different.

I want empanadas.
Oh, brother! I just want cereal with milk!
POPS

My cousins thump in and out of the house, running and shouting.

I want empanadas.
Oh, brother! I just want cereal with milk!
POPS

My cousins thump in and out of the house,
running and shouting.

Yanier and Yudier like to play baseball in the yard.
So far they've broken two flower pots
and our neighbor's window.

Aunt Celia never stops talking and **cooking,**

Abuela chats on the **phone,**

And Cousin Beto

asks everyone

a million questions.

Then everything changes.

"Tia Celia and your cousins are moving to
their own apartment with Abuela,"
Mama tells me one morning.
"Cousin Beto is moving out, too."

Then I find out
that someone else
is coming to

live

in

our

house.

Now our family has gotten
just a little bigger.

"Where
three
can fit,
four
can fit!"

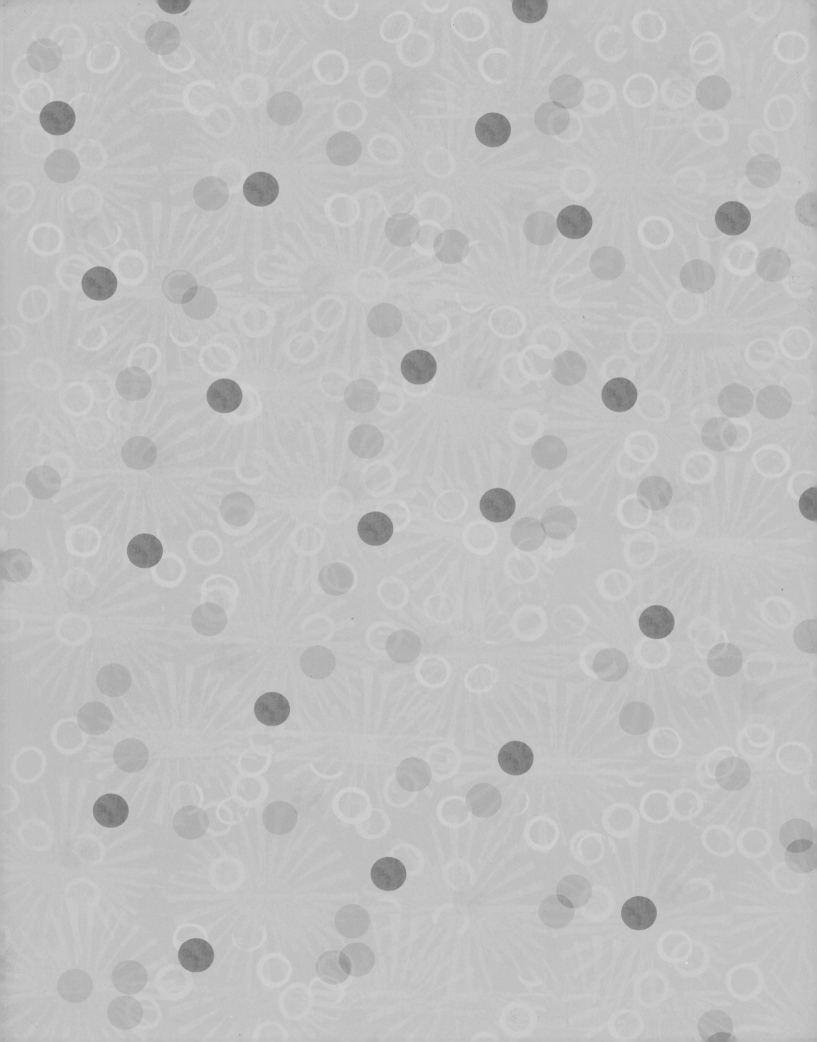